Hi, I'm Mike Peterson. Folks call me Mike, b
As you can probably guess, I wrote this. Nov
guys and gals are all sitting there reading th
your pretty little selves, "why?" Well I'll be h
sure myself! Why is a pretty darn tootingly difficultly quizzically
awkwardly mind-numbingly bloomin awful question to answer now,
ain't it? (the answer to that is yes). Anyway, I reckon time was you
were a-diving deep into these here pages. Maybe see if you can find
you one of those lesser spotted "whys". Go on, dive deep now, you
never know.

Please note (again) there are no prizes for finding any lesser spotted
"whys". Lesser spotted "whys" have no monetary value and cannot
be exchanged for cash, tokens, gifts, gift-cards. If you should happen
to find one, please feel free to jump up and down shouting "JIBERTY
SPLEE, BY LUSTY I DO BELIEVE I HAVE FOUND ONE". Or not
depending on the mood you are in.

Lesser spotted "whys" have been placed at random throughout, I
forgot how many though! Sorry! I think there are about 12.

To
Lyn
Hope you a enjoy
the heargcy

1

Acknowledgements

This book is dedicated to all the lovely people who I know and love!

Extended thanks as always to M Harrison and C Darlington.

And extra special thanks to the following K Bowers, R Buscombe,
C Riley, G Curran, C Lightowler, E Constantine, K Gallimore,
K Konrad, L Cantin, F Larkin, S Hickman-Brown, S Chafer, B Turner
A Elson, C Faulkner, A Faulkner, E K L Hunt, C O'Toole, S O'Toole.

Thanks again of course to Mum and Jim and all my lovely family.
M Rogers, A Melton, P Melton, all the Jones', Matchetts and
Nixons.

In this edition, I have done my best to fill each and every page with
as much "Lunacy and Tripe" as possible! So as to give you lovely folk
as much print per pound! I really do hope you enjoy it and thanks
for looking!

Please note; no offence is intended. Any God, Lord or Deity
mentioned is of my own divinity that I do so believe in.

Please also do note; the bulk of this was written in the space of 4
months, give or take an hour or two! There is no real running order
(it is basically in chronological order), no subversive plots and if you
try to read it backwards, you will not be rewarded with the answer
to the meaning of life! Or Santa's phone number! Sorry what? No
not you sorry! Oh, Satan's phone number!

LUNACY AND TRIPE!

OR

"ECHELONS' REST"

PART II

"SOME HOPE!"

MIKE PETERSON! BY GOLLY, HE'S DONE IT AGAIN!

First published in 2012 by: Ghost Proof Glass Publishing

Words and photograph Copyright 2012 Mike Peterson

ISBN- 978-0-9573867-0-9

Printed and bound in Great Britain by:
Book Printing UK
Remus House
Coltsfoot Drive
Peterborough
PE2 9JX

Other books by the same author include; Echelons' Rest.
That's it sorry! No others. Come on, I've done well to do 2 in 1 year!

AND NOW THE RUNNING ORDER!

(If you like, you can put a little tick next to the ones you like, I have)

9   PRESS 1 FOR ALPHA CENTURI; 2 FOR BETELGEUSE; 3 FOR...

10 TOAST

    REGRET

11 POSSESSSSSSSSED~ ~ ~

    THE 1ST VERSE I EVER WROTE!

12 DAYS AND VEGATABLES

14 THE RIGMAROLE'S TOUR

    THE RIGMAROLE TOURS

15 SERVICE IN HONOUR OF MY JACKET

    SLEEPY, SLEEPY WASTE TIME

17 YOU LOOK FAMILIAR TO ME!

    ABOVE AND BEYOND

18 SHE

19 CAPTAIN SPACETOE!

20 WHAT THE APES SAY!   /

21 GOOD MORNING MR GOD!

22 3D IC

    IMPOLITELY KNOWN AS F@@K!

23 THANKS A FOXING LOT / YOU STUPID OLD BRICK

24 SOCK AND ROLL BABY!!!

    BORIS THE VAMPIRE

25 HAMSTER TIME

    GOING, GOING, GOING, YEH IT'S GONE!

26 TOP-TOY

    NIGHT CAP???

27 HAPPY TIME (SEQUEL (or prequel) TO HAMSTER TIME)

27 HA'S IF!!!

51 LET'S HAVE A PROPPER GANDA!!!

52 HUMP-ME DUMP-ME

LEMMINGS GONE FAR?   /

54 EAT MY LEAVES!

55 FORGOTTEN CROWNS

56 BY NIGHT WE GRACED

AIRBAG HAS BEEN DEEP-PLOYED

57 UP TO YOU GUYS!

58 NAUGHTY CHRISTMAS PART 2   /

59 HEAR ME SQUEAK!!!

WOULD YOU BELIEVE ME?

60 SORRY, WHAT? THINK UP MAN!

HALF AAAAAAGGGGGGGHHHHHSSSSSSSSSD!!!!!!

61 RAIN ANOTHER DAY

62 AH BLESS!

THE DREAMS OF THE LIGHT BRIGADE

63 DREAMJA VU

SOS?

64 FUNKY ZOO PART TWO! GET DOWN!!!

CUT SHORT

65 THE SING-A-SAURUS 12" REMIX (not available in any shops)

66 I CAN'T ROLL YOU

CLICKITY FIX!!!

67 NO WAIT, I FORGET!

68 CALLING DENTIST CARLY

I'M FOREVER PUSHING PENNIES

69 FREE FALLING

FLOWER POWER

YOU BET I WILL

70 SATANS WHY?

LORDS A-WHY?

Please do not attempt to tick your favourites if you are on one of
those electronic book thingies! You know what I'm on about.
I will not be held responsible for the mess it makes if you do!

PRESS 1 FOR ALPHA CENTURI; 2 FOR BETELGEUSE; 3 FOR...

We look out at space and wonder?
"Are we really all alone?"
Will we ever get a call or text
From beyond our little home?
Vast Radar installations
Eves drop the cosmic sky
Trying to catch a message
From 'anyone' passing by.
Are we wasting time?
Trying to contact stars
Or merely seeking comfort
In telling 'them' where we are?
For years we've tried to say "hello"
From prayers to modern apps
We've even sent directions
On some A-Z space maps
Maybe 'they're' just ignorant
"Have got too much to do"
Or maybe they heard us long ago
But have seen our colours true!
But who's to say
Somewhere out there
Beyond our sky so blue
A lonely little alien
Simply can't get through!

"SORRY, THE NUMBER YOU HAVE DIALED HAS NOT BEEN
RECOGNISED. PLEASE HANG UP AND TRY AGAIN! SORRY, THE..."

It really is amazing where inspiration comes from. Not so where perspiration comes from though! That last little one about the lonely alien (poor chap), was inspired by a picture of a satellite! Well it wouldn't have been a picture of a pair of slippers would it?

TOAST

Nicely warm
Like a fresh piece of toast
Or some boil in the bag kippers
That is how my tootsies feel
When I wear my fluffy slippers.

Ok, I know, it was crap! Just diversifying a bit, I'll get back on track now.

REGRET

Sometimes it's hard to say goodbye
And leave a dear friend
When things go wrong
Sometimes it's hard to say "ok, you are right"
Admit defeat
When you know you were right all along
But if friends are who they say
The only thing left behind
Is a brief moment of history
And a chance to make up time.

Ok, the next one is one of my favourites! Hope you like it to!

POSSESSSSSSSSED~ ~ ~

Take from me this Poets heart
That beats like drums half dead
Squeeze from it last ounce of life
Till life is all but bled
Fly a flag of solitude
From where it once beat strong
And pave a path to Tyranny
From where it all went wrong
This heart so cruel
Will beat subdued
Never will it rest
As it crawls through life
Enraged in spite
And twists
Like snakes
Possessed

MOVES LIKE PASSION 31ST 3RD 12

THIS IS THE 1ST VERSE I EVER WROTE, WHEN I WAS 8 (I THINK).

Inside this bin is a rusty old tin
And old toy car, a broken guitar
And some tea time scraps that attract cats
So keep the lid on tight
Especially at night
Because that's when the cats come in
To raid your bin.

DAYS AND VEGATABLES

I awoke, it was late. As to whether or not it was day or night is irrelevant, it was just late. Through the darkness a large orange ball of fire was suspending itself just above the local institute of untamed empty jars of Vaseline. The clock on the wall said "Here, here, it's not in the way of a sprout to constipate a thought". Then without undue care or attention to the surrounding environment, consisting of a cosy little spud in the outer Hybrids, fell off. The wall that is! Back to the plot! What a waste of time, 3 hours and six days after finally getting out of bed I find nothing is ever as it is, was or has ever has been. Am I in the wrong story here? So many planes, so many planes. And I want them all. Resist thy temptation laddie, for yours is not to attend to the Ottoman. Nor the great vines of peas that once so lusciously paraded naked in all their glory to the tune of "Whistle not the key is baked". A small cluster of things clustered in a way that only things of that nature can cluster. The path now I must take will change back to the way so as not to step on said clustered things. Else I may disengage something from its' rightful resting station. A cabbage rests wearily its' tungsten grip on life, with the imminent prospect of global warming on a bed pan scale. Reluctant, it wilfully throws itself beneath the onslaught of a swarm of intelligent wingbeans. In not knowing what it didn't, nor ever did not know, in the first place, this is going to be one messed up cabbage. Aside from the placid coming and coming again, maybe for dinner sometime, if not a quick sandwich is worth 8 against a kipper. Not, not you've got the wrong end of the stick on the kipper. And that is in, by any way, no means a red herring. My slippers, all along they were never near. No wonder traction was forced and less pliable. It's a crazy world we live in. For one man to find happiness in willing, willing must be a bit fucking stupid. As I have never heard a

12

thousand times a second the mighty thrashing of leather against the chic elegant backdrop of rose tinted turnips, wanting for nothing. Slash, slash! Incompetent maybe! Incontinent?? Answers on a carrier pigeon labelled for Easy Street will not arrive in time for Easter. Bad luck Santa. Gleefully I watched as amidst the trees the carrots played happily. Unaware as the hunger driven, lesser spotted, stays in so as not to miss a thing Sooopie, craft-fully makes plans as to rid the planes, so many planes, can I have them? Junctions in time often succumb to a build up of fag-butts, thus sssslllllowing on a thrip-ne-bit. We forthwith apologise for any garments left in the changing rooms alone. Spooky isn't it? Once again I was cheated on the cereal, milk is no substitute for a player sent off in the third half, due to lack of Government funding. The Red Card means one thing and two if it has a fudge. You're out of here buddy! Pack 3 days worth of pancakes, then go! Oh no! The carrot fell over. Narrowly missing the dog dirt. Instead choosing to land in the Sooopie shit. What will his mother say? You're no carrot of mine, Sonny Bob! Can I get a real job these days? Taking vaccinations is fine if you have the time and money. After pressing through such a mountain of old rickshaws. Hay; what the hell, they get you there. Just in time to miss the last one after only allowing two before hand to pass by unaware after it had gone. Sneaky, sneaky! It's at times like this I think "what the hell was tomorrow about?" Back to bed for now. What a lovely day!

I hope you enjoyed reading my first ever story. If you like you can now play a game where-by, who ever tallies up the most amount of vegetables named in above text wins. Depending on how many people are with you depends on how many hours of fun you have.

THE RIGMAROLE'S TOUR

The Rigmarole
On his way back home
Stopped at a quarter past eight
Due north heading south
With his pipe in his mouth
Running slowly because he was late
By chance he did catch
The first bus and the last
To the stop from where once he had come
And took a quick tour
Of things seen before
And ended up early back home

THE RIGMAROLE TOURS

The Rigmarole
Is a wise old mole
Who lives in Clever Clogs Woods!
He likes to read all sorts of stuff
And has hundreds and hundreds of books
But what he really loves to do
Is pack up all his cases
And drive his double-decker bus
To lots of different places
He has lots of friends he likes to see
And is always making more
So pack some lunch, jump aboard
And join the Rigmarole's tour

SERVICE IN HONOUR OF MY JACKET

LAID TO REST 8TH JULY, IN THE YEAR OF OUR LORD

NINTEEN HUNDRED AND NINETY SIX

Minister in charge of sermon: Carl. *

Friends, we are gathered here together on this evening to lay to rest, a part of our friends life, in order that it will not be forgotten.

For seven long years this jacket has done its duty, come rain or shine, snow or hail, day or night, etc, etc, etc. And in its time, Yay let it be known, has only required the need to be washed, on no more than; not six, not five, nay lad not even four. In its time on this mortal planet, this here jacket has seen the light of the washing machine (ie, the light that indicates that the machine is in use) on no more than three, I repeat, three occasions. Which is pretty good going by my book! Unfortunately, though, time did take its toll, and lesser members of our society, could not accept the relationship between jacket and man. Nor the fact that it was fucking filthy. Nor so the fact that to wash such a jacket, would have been blasphemy. And Yay let it be known, that it is as a result of these soulless creatures, that you are stood here today.

Though it is the request of ***, the owner of this fine piece of Denim art, that no man, woman or child shall feel anger toward said members of society. Therefore a wake shall take place shortly after, in which large quantities of ale will be consumed. Cucumber sandwiches will also be served.

Now I will ask, please, for a moments silence. During which time this tree will be planted, as a reminder to future generations. Of such a magnificent Jacket.

NOT SPOKEN.

Following the minutes silence a twenty one gun salute will sound. For all to hear. Providing we can get twenty one guns.

SPOKEN.

All that now remains, is to cast this small reminder to the ground. Earth to earth, ashes to ashes, dust to dust. Thank you for all attending. Let us now get well and truly trollied.

MLP 5/7/96

*In most cases I have left out names, I have made an exception to the above as Carl was a very dear friend and a great laugh. Wishing you well mate whatever you are doing! This event did take place!!!

SLEEPY, SLEEPY WASTE TIME

Why dream when you're awake
What a pointless waste of time
Do it while you're sleeping
Or you'll waste half your life

Phew! Thanks to my eagle like eyes, you don't have 2 copies of above verse. Remember; proof reading pays off kids!!!

YOU LOOK FAMILIAR TO ME!

You are a cat
My little cat
And I love you for that
And that is that!

My cat is great, she really is, to the extent that I don't look at her as a pet, more as my Familiar. And having, in the past, been accused of being a Witch, it can't be more fitting really, can it?

ABOVE AND BEYOND

"Good Lord! We can't leave you alone for two minutes, can we?"
"Oh come on, it has been nearly two hundred thousand years."
"Yes, significant progress!"
"Hey it's not my fault they chose to go their own way. And remember, it was your idea. Give them identity; give them individuality, spontaneity, character. My, hasn't it proved successful?"
"All right, we're not here to argue, we just want the results."
"Yes, plain and simple please, is it worth our while carrying on?"
"Well, the atmospheres' shot, resources are low and, they're still there. Personally myself, I think just a little more time may be of benefit, to us. If only to see how they end it. If you think about it, it might save us the effort."
"Yes, good thinking. Ok, we'll give them another fifty years, see what happens!"
"If they don't, we will, Eh!"
"Exactly! After all, it only took six days to create."

SHE

She's no mind of her own
She's too busy stealing others
She's like a preacher on heat
Converting all the lovers
Blue murder she screams
If she can't get her way
And it's never her fault
Who's to blame? I cannot say!
Don't worry
You're not the first
To wet her appetite
Quench her thirst
She's no love of her own
She thinks it's all second rating
Spare no thought for her
Amidst your dirty masturbating
She'll take a one night stand
Any time
She'll be your all night lover
For a lager and lime
Don't worry
You are not her love
She'll be rid of you
When the sun comes up
She's no style of her own
It's all cut from a magazine
Last years' ideas
She's the cat without the cream
What she'll do to you

Is no-one's guess
She just likes to do
What she does best

7/1/97. Who is she? Je, ne sai.

CAPTAIN SPACETOE!

Captain Spacetoe
He is great
He is here to save the day
Fighting all the nasty scum
Flying off into the sun
He is brave
And really tough
Beating all the villains up
In his spaceship
Out in space
Captain Spacetoe
He is dead good!

31 MARCH 12

Me writing this much in such a short space of time means one of
two things; by Jobe, I'm bloody good, or, I'm having a slight mental
breakdown! It happens from time to time, don't worry, I'll be ok
soon. Probably by the end of this book! Flippity-squibilty-squat

Board games, so called because after 5 minutes, I'm bored!!!

WHAT THE APES SAY!

Hello and welcome to a special edition of "What the Apes Say". For this part, a group of genetically engineered, highly intelligent apes were used as a test audience for this book. Here is what some of them had to say;

"I say old chap, bravo! Top marks all round, what!"

"Mr Peterson seems so very able to convey his inner thoughts and feelings onto paper, in a wonderful array of words and phrases"

"I must admit, this boy has talent. True, some of it is still a little bit rough around the edges, but on the whole, this is a rather fine read"

Now for this part, we used genetically engineered, slightly less intelligent apes. Here's what they had to say;

"OOO! It'll suck your socks off"

"I think I'd understand it better if I was a monkey"

"I like chips"

"It's crap"

"When do we get paid?"

All the monkeys were released back to the wild after this exercise. One chose not to go and has managed to secure a record deal.

GOOD MORNING MR GOD!

Who can teach creation?
Write it on a page
Hand out inspiration
Show the class New Wave!
Are ideas copied?
Filed for later dates?
Are they good for nothing?
Just re-released mistakes
Can this stuff be taught?
Or is it gift or curse?
Bouncing off ideas
Until ideas burst
The writings on the wall
But the wall's a half done job
So one last thought
On how it's taught
Who on earth
Taught God?

Just below are a couple of lines that didn't make it into above. They
are a bit naff, don't you think??? Don't you? Hmm!!!

Is it something that can be done?
If you teach me your way of write
The writings on the wall
If you can read then it's your job

If you want you can rearrange them back in somewhere.

3D IC

Break the barriers of reality
Fulfil your wildest dreams
See the world and beyond with your own eyes
Not from a TV screen
Excel in excellence
Smash through all boundaries
Unlock your deepest and darkest desires
Go on,
Turn the keys!

IMPOLITELY KNOWN AS F@@K!

Beep is a sound
So often heard
It gives us a warning
And covers up words
Oh "BEEP" to this
And "BEEP" to that
But try keeping your "BEEP"
Under your hat!

Other titles that I considered for this book included
"Have you read my other book "Echelons' Rest?"
"My other book is quite good, by all accounts"
"Who let the Dog out?"
 "book22 (Autosaved)"
"Bissen Sie Die Satsumas, Schnell, Schnell!"
"I like Eggs but Prefer Dinghies"

THANKS A FOXING LOT

A Fox did go the docs
With a really painful ache
"Oh Doc" said Fox "please help me out"
"Whatever should I take?"
Doc said
"For fox ache take these pills
  After having food"
To which Fox replied
"Thanks a lot
  There's no need to be rude!"

YOU STUPID OLD BRICK

In an age old town in days gone by
Where folks were a little bit thick
And the highest IQ that could be raised
Belonged to a broken brick
The locals quizzed their knowledge
With a game of hide and seek
And made it in to college
If they found themselves
Within a week

Right, just to set the record straight; this page once had a song
called "You Bet I can Sigh!" on it. Being that it wasn't really my song
to start off with (I re-wrote the lyrics) I thought it was a cop out! So
2 brand new ones were drafted in to replace it!

SOCK AND ROLL BABY!!!

I like sausage rolls
So put another batch
In the oven baby
I like sausage rolls
27 minutes
On gas mark 3

(ages ago, no idea of date. Sorry peeps)

BORIS THE VAMPIRE

Prepping his fangs
So precise, no missed chance
To comfortably feed his fill
Boris the Vampire
Licks his white lips
Before engaging his kill
Armed like a demon
With teeth sharp as blades
And stealth like
Skilled ninja cats
And a bottle of sauce
To top his main course
Of French Fries
And quick deep fried sprats

MY LIFE POURS 3RD OF APRIL AND IT IS STILL 2012!

HAMSTER TIME

In writing rhymes
I sometimes find
It's often hard
To change the time
Of when the rhyme
 Rhymes with the line
And when it's right
To change the time
Of the word that takes
The pre read line
And makes it sound
Like it should rhyme
It really is a cursing crime
Trying to change
The rhyming rhyme
STOP!
Hamster time?

3RD April 12, AGAIN!!!

GOING, GOING, GOING, YEH IT'S GONE!

And now my mind is going
I'm forgetting what I'm knowing
I just can't seem,,,,,,,,,,,,,,, to ,,,,,,,,,,concentrate no more
And faces from my past
Look back at me and laugh
"Hay there, what ya doin?"

TOP-TOY

Boldly going forward
Beyond that which is out of touch
For the simple thing you ask
Ask yourself "do I ask too much?"
True to form, it may seem
You have lost your favourite toy
And you can't replace the feeling
That gave you so much joy
But don't deny yourself
Because you feel unsure
If you like someone, they may like you
And if you try, you may find
You may both like some more.

NIGHT CAP???

Maybe someday soon
You'll figure out
What it means to dream
What it's all about
Until then I'm sure
You'll sleep sound in your bed
With your empty thoughts
In your empty head

Sorry, really have no idea when I did these. Doesn't really matter
though does it? If it does bother you, please let me know. Thanks!
Xxx

HAPPY TIME (SEQUEL (or prequel) TO HAMSTER TIME)

My sense of mind depleted
Ignorance somewhat subdued
Forgive me what was said
If it seemed to be somewhat rude
As you may have grasped already
My writing is of the type
The one of which
You either love or loathe
Or totally dislike
I'm not sure, it's hard to tell
But believe these last few lines
It's hard to please all of you folks
All at once and all the time!

HA'S IF!!!

It's so concise
On every station
Media plugged information
Amidst party political broadcasts
Then make the most
Of a game show host
Rest at ease
With a cup of tea
It's so cheap these days
To get an honest laugh.

May I delve into the depths of your smarty-pants?

TICK

Turn around
And show your face
Tempt the past
With loving grace
So softly sung
Your haunting song
It will grace the time
That you belong
And when your time
Like songs are sung
Then you'll know
Your time is done.

DRIP!

The sky hangs grey
Looking ill and un-clever
The seasons now ghosts
Of a past not remembered
And the forecasters jobs
Have long since been severed
It's so easy these days
To forecast the weather
All we need say
Is it now rains forever

9TH of April 12

28

boo

Shush now darling
Clear your mind
As we stare into our eyes
Quiet my dear
We won't say a word
For fear we'll spoil surprise

GUN

How lethal is a gun?
Can you analyse its kill
Record in a bar-chart
Its accuracy and skill
Present a clear percentage
Of fatalities and maims
Then write a rave revue
Don't worry about the names
How lethal is a gun?
I can give you a rough figure
The answer is zero
It can't pull its own trigger.

12TH 4th 12

Many thanks to Poetry24 for publishing "Gun" on the 7th June 12.

To the really nice couple parked up on the Old Dock Road, thanks for the offer but it was a bit bloody cold!

OLD FAITHFUL!

Off she did chuff
Down the rusty old line
To her next destination
Coughing out smoke
Like a chesty old bloke
Who'd forgotten his medication!
Passing the points
Past the signal man's box
On time, not a second to loose
Gathering pace
And banishing haste
With whistles and chuffs and choo-choos
She reaches on time
The end of the line
And stops for a quick
Catch of breath
Then with carriages full
With a peep and a toot
Old Faithful sets off again.

Oh yes, it's the 10th of April! I like this day!

BENT RULER

A poem doesn't have to rhyme
Don't for a minute think that is the case
As you can see
In this one!

DICKY BROWN

Ow, didley folks? Dick Brown here. How's yer chestnuts? Word has it, a gardening chum of mine writes, somewhat, naughty novels. Ooo-er!!! Bet you didn't know, though, that I beat him to it? Had a bit of trouble with mine though, as me old typewriter started cocking up and going down. Here's an extract.

"Would you like to sack my duck?" Bernard asked.

"Oh I'd love to" Said Beryl. "I love sacking ducks!"

"I'm sure you do. I bet you sack like a real pro"

And with that, Bernard released his big, hefty duck. It stood tall and proud and somewhat menacing inches from her face!

"Oh my!" exclaimed Beryl. "I don't think I've ever seen a duck that big before. Where do I start?"

"Try locking its bill" Bernard said.

Beryl leant forward and gently locked its bill. Then, she locked it all over, making sure she locked everywhere. Meanwhile, Bernard moaned, as he watched his duck completely disappear.

"Do you like jazz?" Bernard sighed

"Oh I love jazz!" cooed Beryl.

And with that, Bernard pumped the room full of jazz. In all directions, some bounced off the walls and ceiling while some caught Beryl's ears straight away.

"What shall we do with your duck now Bernard?" Beryl asked, as it started flapping.

"Well!" said Bernard, "if you turn round and open your shutter, I'll shove him in there".

Not sure about blue, my mobile phone is that old, it has yellow tooth.

THE STRINGS

Walk on with strings
Pulled from above
Dance a little dance
Go through the day
Looking for love
Take a little chance
Suddenly find
That your strings are all tied
In a web of such sweet divine bliss
Then collapse with a sigh
Trying to unwind
Ten thousand
How did it come to this?

Writers Log; page date 11th April 2012. Just got up!

ANYTHING ON?

Same old stuff
There's nothing new
Pick something up
While flicking through?
So what's next?
Who's decision?
Turn it off
End transmission!

Please note; No keys were harmed in the making of this book!

NICE! VERY NICE!!!

Busy making curry
Stinking the whole house through
Lamb Rogan Josh
Tikka and Vindaloo
I like making curries
They are really nice
Nicely topped off with poppadoms
And lots of pilau rice!

Without doubt my favourite food group! Mmm Madras!!!

WITCH EVER WEIGH YEW LOOK, IT'S ALL COMPLETELY WROTE

If you put the wrong words
In the write plaice
The read can be very Miss Red
Four examples, I'm drawn
Knot to tie my own horn
About rabbits and how they are bread
Rabbit sandwich divine
I prefer rabbit pye
But my knowledge of pye
Is so paw
And as two whom I should sea
To resolve mystery
I can't really say four shore!

3 hard days of writing went into the above folks! Are ya happy?

WHICH WITCH DIDN'T GO TO IPSWICH?

Winding her way
With the wind in her hair
On a bicycle made for nineteen
Winslay the Witch
Wound her way
Round the towns
From Penzance to East Aberdeen
Picking up friends
From start to end
Her tour covered much of the land
And they stopped off at pubs
For some pints and some lunch
It was such a weird witch gang
There was
Petrlua from Penzance
Brendina from Bath
Debnah from north of Dundee
Heffna from Hasting
Shorna from Slough
And Trix from the town of Torquay
Katrina from Kent
Carrie of Crew
Lousy of Lytham St Anne
Ettie of East Cowes
Big-Chigs from Brighouse
And Franken from Fakenham
Listless form Leicester
Dang from Manchester
Belle-Hay-Bie from Ball Haye Green

Marta from Manley
Helga of Hanley
And Andraya from East Aberdeen
Last but not least
As they headed off East
They remembered that they had forgotten
So they spun it around
And headed back down
To pick up Wilton
From Frinton and Walton
Now if you'd kept pace
In this wayward witch race
You'd see they had full score plus one
And past East Aberdeen
Having only nineteen
All but one seat had gone
Still with Wilton to go
Winslay thought with an "OH!"
 "Oh I've left my broom in the car
 And the car's in Penzance
 So I'll just take my chance
 And sit on the handle bars!"

Katy this one is for you! x

BY JOBE SAYS I, TIS APRIL 10TH!!! HOOZAH!!!

This one was amended after a small challenge was accepted, by me!
I really should stop doing it! "Hey Mike, run 30miles!" "Duh ok!"

PENNING FOR GOLD

Sat without thought
And nothing to write
My mind is an empty old hole
Fingers lay idle
Tap-tapping away
Ideas as rare as old gold
My pen's in the stream
Penning away
But the gold is reluctant to show
So I'll give you this rhyme
And apologise
For not giving your
Full quota gold

GOLD STRUCK APRIL 17TH-Y-ALL!

WOULD YOU!

Would you buy a watch?
That told second hand time
Or sing an old song
Without any rhyme
Paint a rainbow filled sky
With drab shades of grey
Put off tomorrow
What you've not done today!

Written April 18th, started many moons ago! I was busy! Honest!

SLEEP

Ellah Gurhella
Lay there and wept
The trees asked for rain
And the porch had been swept
Of life, she caught a confused peep
Then drifted softly off to sleep
How years roll by
Now she sat
Sat there bemused
The trees were strong green
And the porch was unused
Again she caught that confused peep
Then took herself off
Off to sleep
How years draw close
Now once again, there she lay
The trees had new rings
She had only a day
And in that day
That confused peep
That baffled her
Throughout her keep
Revealed itself
And took her off
Took her off to sleep....

Pn: El-lah Gore-hel-lah

This has taken years to complete! Date today 16th 4th 12.

AND NOW THE CIRCUS COMES TO TOWN!!! ARRIVAL!

A grumbling monster
Sixty foot long
Trundled and mumbled
Through the night
It didn't know where it was to go
Or the meaning of the word "quiet"
It just pressed on, regardless
Grinding ground
Without a care
And belching out
Thick clogging smog
That squeezed life
Out of the air
A truck of sorts?
Maybe once!
Difficult to say
It now looked more organic
In a strange obscene way
But looks did not besiege it
The last thing on its "mind"
It did its job
And did it well
Getting there on time!
Carrying its cargo
Of life beyond remorse
This surrogate metal mother
This strange truck of sorts

SO, SO FLO! OR, MUCH ADO ABOUT SCOFFING!

Now behold the many folds
Of the one they call "Five Tonne Flo!"
This grotesque beast is so obese
She's never seen her toes
All day she sits, festering
In squalor beyond disgust
Wedged in an old hospital bed
Reinforced with weld
And eaten away by rust
Daily she's fed
By her husband Reg
A creature as thin as a stick
A filthy pervert
Who relishes dirt!
And shags like a dog
With three dicks
But he keeps alive
His rewarding prize
She brings in the cash
Would he be sad if she died?
My friend, you're having a laugh
She's a one woman freak-show
All dignified privacy gone
And like the food going in her mouth
Her show must go on and on
Any sense of morals
And any sense of pride
Have so, so long been banished
Beneath the sheets

So, so caked with grime
Her complexion has past gruesome
All justice to her size
And her stench is overwhelming
Even flies pass her by
But her heart is in the right place
Even though it's not much use
She's kept alive with electric wire
Whilst her blood is pumped through tubes

TICKLE TIME!

One, two
Look at their shoes
Three, four
They're not on the floor?
Five, six
They can't half kick!
Seven, eight
Right in your face!
Laugh all you like
You'll soon change your tune
The Macabre Clowns are in town
They'll slaughter your laughter
Into the hereafter
As laughter is muffled and drowned
So quick with the jokes
And willing to choke
Decapitate and devour
They'll leave an audience
All "stitched" up

Within their Carnage Hour
To amuse and abuse their hapless crowd
They use such lovely props
Like rubber knives made of steel
And cuffs you can't unlock
And what can rattle better
Than the tail of a snake?
A snake with its rattle
Mere inches from your face
And last but least
They'll paint your face
In layered shades of dull
As they peel back the layers
To reveal your screaming skull
Now if your sides are still intact
With 60 minutes past
They'll gladly slice you
Top to toe
And give you back your cash

(Ok, you have probably guessed! I don't like clowns (I did mention in my last book (did you read it?)). I have nothing against them; they just scare the crap out of me!)

If you were a dinosaur, which one would you be; Diplodocus, Tyrannosaurus, Triceratops, Brontosaurus, Allosaurus, Stegosaurus, other? And why?

MAP APP!

On his way to the chiropodist
A lost hippopotamus
Stopped and asked a wily baboon
"By chance do you know?
  Which way I should go
  I really must get there by two
  I'm running quite late
  And my feet hurt like ache
  Due to two pairs of ill fitting shoes"
The baboon with a frown
Looked up and looked down
Shook his head
Then spoke like a short cross lit fuse
  "I'm sorry dear chap
  I can't read a map
  And hippos should never wear shoes!"

Poor hippo, I don't know if he got there in the end. I do hope so!
That baboon was a bit nasty wasn't he?

The hippo did get there in the end, on the 19th of April. AWWW!

To the nice people who make underpants; please put the "I made
these" label on the back, not the side! It confused me a bit last
night! Thank you!

I tried writing pottery once, didn't half make a mess.

WHITER THAN?

Poor Snow White did not feel good
She really felt unwell
"Oh Lord" she thought
 "I bet that bitch, the Wicked Witch, Has put me under a spell"
At first she felt Happy
She felt Happy from top to toe
But she then moved to Sleepy
And Happy had to go!
Sleepy she felt for a while
As the time ticked by on the clock
Then she started feeling Sneezy
So she got a hold of Doc
Doc gave her a good once over
Did her front and behind
Told her to swallow his magical juice
And told her she was fine
Now she really did feel Happy
Vibrant and pumped up on pace
But she came back down
With such a frown
And Grumpy came over her face
Now I bet you've all been thinking
"Snow White's a dirty bitch"
But she was at home, all alone
The dwarfs were out _____ the Witch!

(I'll let you fill the blank in! Ooo, saucy!)
Wrote this 29th April! Good month for writing! Did about 30ish!

DICK-A-DOODLE-DOO!!!

Goldilocks
She so loves cocks
Of any shape and size
Especially the massive ones
They bring tears to her eyes
She'll play with them all day long
Until they reach their peak
And then she'll stroke them softly
And kiss them on the beak

ACCESS DENIED!!!

We get confused
It's what we do
Us silly human beings
We lose the plot
Say we forgot
The nature of our meaning
And come our time
If we're denied
Everlasting rest
We'll shout and scream
At a greater being
And claim we did our best

Both of above were born on the 9th of May 12! Happy Birthday Guys!

NEG-BOMB NUMBER 1

Don't worry if you wake one morn to find you have dreamt too far above your true potential! DREAMS AREN'T REAL! And nice "get back to sleep quick" tablets are available from most shops these days!

Definition of a NEG-BOMB; when some incredibly miserable sausage, inadvertently or not, really pee's on your happily, brightly polished, little toy town parade and makes you feel like poo. To which your response would be "for fox ache, stop dropping NEG-BOMBS you miserable sausage".

RENT-A-TROLL

My name is Crumpled Foreskin
And I hide in dirty holes
I don't like Goblin Fairies
But I love Goblin Trolls
Goblin Trolls are great
They are big and strong and,,,,
Hang on, hang on, wait a minute
What do you think I meant?
Oooooooooh! (Long pause for effect here chaps! Go on then)
Well, somebody's got to do it
And it does help pay the rent! Boom, boom!

I'm not interested in living the dream. I find it's more fun trying to slaughter the nightmare! Come on you bstd!!!

You must be sick of me putting the dates at the end of every single bloody verse I create! You're not! Oh well then, that last one "Rent-A-Troll" was written 15th May 2012. At 20.20pm!!! Not long till my birthday. YIPPEE!!!

DAFT!

Erbert O-Krackers was daft
As daft as a bag of old cats
He had an old watch
That told the wrong time
So at quarter to three
It was twenty past nine
No wonder Erbert
Was never on time
Daft, daft, daft
He bought a bike
But the front wheel was gone
And he looked such a sight
Trying to ride it back home
 Doing a wheelie
On one wheel alone
Daft, daft, daft
The paper he bought
Told last weeks' news
He had a pair of two left shoes
In a one horse race
He would surely loose
Daft, daft, daft.

HARK! THE HERALD ANGEL SCREECH!!!

My fingers are joyful and happy
Dancing around
Like the first lambs of spring
My mind is engaged in a poetic wave
By-jolly I think I may sing!
But hark this hapless angel
Steer clear of its voice
Cover your ears
Run in fear
It's a bloody awful noise
"IF YOU'RE GOING, TO SANDRAS' DISCO!"

BUTTERFINGERS

If the world is at our fingertips
How come so much is out of our grasp?
If the future is yet to come
How come we are catching up with our past?
Have we learnt to sprint?
Before we really learnt to walk!
Told all of our tales
Before we could even talk
Placed ourselves upon a pinnacle
Graced ourselves beyond all mighty
Have we really lost our grasp?
Or do we need to hold on more tightly?

It's the sunny, funny, smiley, happy sunshine gang!!! Yea

ALL THE FUN OF THE PHWOOOOOAR!!!

At the "Filthy Fair" of no despair
The rides are somewhat rude
And adult fun
Comes in tonnes
All smutilly glazed with crude
So park your arse
On the Dogging Cars
And be bumped hard from behind
Or flick your stick
At Hook-a-Dick
And grab yourself a prize
Then scare your wits
To a stage past shits
In the ghastly House of Mingers
These gruesome gals
With toothless smiles
And smells beyond what lingers
Will happily ride your failing pride
To stage a beyond just aching
Then wipe you clean
With some Mr Shine
And a cloth that's nicely caking
So come along all Guys and Gals
The Deecups need a-ridin
And how the hell they ring that bell
Is somewhat quite surprising!!!
"DING DONG!"

THREAD BARE!

It's hard to believe
That the threads that we weave
Can ware so thin
And then break
And all of the while
A comforting smile
Hides the pain
That we're willing
To take

MAN THE LIEFBOATS

Now your cans have all been kicked
And your battleship is sunk
And you just can't speak the truth
Unless you're blind stinking drunk
And you're walking on thin ice
With the sunshine beating down
Thinking what will crack first
Is it safer to drown?
In an ocean of feelings
Emotions capsized
In a mind without reason
What is truth?
Untold lies!

A good fart should sound like a clumsy old dump truck starting up.
And smell like beef and turnip soup. Fact! Maybe a bit damp as well.

ALL FIVE SENSELESS

I'm coming to get you!
There's nowhere you can hide
This world just isn't big enough
For my beady little eyes
There are no shadows' dark enough
No caves so deep
And I've got my beady nose on you
When I am asleep
There is no perfume strong enough
No spray so bold
And I've got my beady ears on you
When I have a cold
There are no sounds loud enough
No BOOMS or BANGS or RIOTS
And I've got my beady fingers on you
When you're being quite
There's no place hot enough
I don't care about chilly ice
But after that I'm rather stuck
Because you don't taste very nice. Pah!

Here's to sentimentality! It's great, but it won't put food on the table! Just sell that stuff! Especially that turny, spinny round puzzle cube, you will never bloody solve it! You've been trying for how many years now? Let it go!

Even more words that I find funny; skid marks, plop, trump, plump

LET'S HAVE A PROPPER GANDA!!!

Don't tag me with lines untrue
Or hate me out of spite
Keep your lashing tongue within
And banners out of sight
If propaganda fuels your fire
Then kindly douse your flames
And revel in your own self worth
Before destroying names
You paint your pictures
With a brush you don't know how to use
Then use your art with ignorance
In a school of useless fools
My, my you are so clever
With your strength of numbers, fear and hate
But my sides better than your side
But what's it going to take?

The above little rhyme has had a couple of modifications throughout the years. Words put in, words taken out, in, out, in, out, you get the idea. And no, I'm not doing the Hokey-Cokey!!!

People, it is my sad duty to inform you, that the Sunny, Funny, Smiley, Happy Sunshine gang from a couple of pages ago, have spilt-up and gone their separate ways. They told me there were no hard feelings within the group, they just needed time out.

Do any of you nice people out there have a recipe for ice cubes at all?

Ok folks, I know what you have all been wondering. It's been playing on your minds for years hasn't it? Niggling away since the first time you ever heard it; Humpty Dumpty, did he fall or was he pushed? Well now, it just so happens that I may be able, to once and for all, settle this age old debate. And put your eggy minds at ease! With this next little number.

HUMP-ME DUMP-ME

Humpty Dumpty climbed up the wall
And peeped over the other side
He saw lots of odd things going on
And they made Humpty smile
He saw such sights, the likes of which
He'd never seen before
And as he looked harder
He saw more, and more and more
He saw,
Old Mother Hubbard
Bent over her cupboard
Getting a nice big bone
For her little dog Mack
Who needed a snack
Please don't lower the tone
And Jill's other half Jack
Was flat on his back
After trying to fill her bucket
But to no avail
Jill has such a big pale
So he sacked it
And told her to suck it

And Christopher Robbins'
Head was a-bobbin
Just outside the palace
The daft old turd
Had slightly misheard
The order to "go down with Alice"
Deep in the wood
Red Riding Hood
Had been startled by the Wolf
After questioning size "are they really that big?"
To her surprise
He really made her gulp!
Now with all this excess
I'm sure you can guess
Humpty's mind was not on the ball
And finding that things were getting quite hard
Is the reason
He fell off the wall

Later on in this book, as the tripe unfolds, you will come across the
child friendly version of this egg based verse. Eggs are ace!

LEMMINGS' GONE FAR?

The Lemmings left home after breakfast
And said they'd be back before bed
But they lost their way
Around midday
And headed towards Beachy Head

EAT MY LEAVES!

An apple a day may keep the Doctor at bay
But it sealed all mankind's fate
Eve happily crunched
From the forbidden bunch
On advice from a treacherous snake
Now just think for a tick
Had she not been so quick
To cause such a great divide
Would the world still be,
In harmony
And still wearing our leaves with pride!

Here is a list of words that you should try to avoid, if you decide you would like to write poetry; night, arse, purple, orange, toffee, staple, divine, whale, concoction, rudimentary, echelon.

If at this stage of the book, you are thinking "what the hell have I bought here?" don't worry! This book also has a number of handy little practical apps to warrant how much you paid! They are thus;

App 1, fix that wonky chair or table in the blink of an eye!
App 2, someone used the last bit of toilet paper? No fear!
App 3, in need of some kindling to get that fire started? TA-DA!
App 4, Oh no! You've forgotten someone's birthday, but you don't like them anyway. Say no more!!!

Please do not try to use these apps if you are reading this on one of those electronic book thingies! Thanks!

FORGOTTEN CROWNS

I went to see a procession yesterday
Of the summer Kings and Queens
On the back of brightly coloured trucks
Oh wait, that was a long lost childhood dream.
True, something did go past
With pomp and pretentious flare
But as sterile as a needle
No magic in the air.
No paper folded flowers
Or bunting hung on string
No children waving frantically
And certainly no Queen or King.
Instead a media convoy
Of mobile TV sets
With models smiling warmly
Well, trying to do their best
A sad state of affairs
The global moguls on parade
Telling us what we should buy
As we looked on and waved
But times are hard these days
And most have hit the skids
So to all you corporate fat cats
Oh, and the Health and Safety crowd
Just for once dismiss your crowns
And reinstate the kids.

Sweaty chocolate pops! No idea sorry!

BY NIGHT WE GRACED

We graced the sky
As best we could
With colours from our hearts
We asked the sun to rise each morn
And banish cold and dark
To the stars we said
"Sparkle bright, make patterns
 Fit for Queens"
Whilst the moon was asked
The tricky task
Of watching over dreams
Then we added a dash of colour
The rainbows were our touch
So you would forgive us for the rain
We can only do so much!

AIRBAG HAS BEEN DEEP-PLOYED

Farther Slee P O'feel nodded off at the wheel
And hit a shop full of porn
Where he woke with blind fear
A bung in his rear
And a rubber doll blowing his horn
Honk, honk!

Oh Innuendo, where would we be without you? Uranus maybe! See,
it still makes you titter like a school kid. I just wrote tit as well! If you
are a bit prudish, you may as well ditch this book now.

UP TO YOU GUYS!

Where's the greatest place on earth?
      !
Where pound for pound you'll get your worth!
      !
Where the locals always bid good morn
With a friendly welcome nice and warm
And the gardens boast the greenest lawn
It's   !
Where the smiles are always two for one
You can drive a dinghy down the
And meet the mighty
It's   ,
Yes   ,
Oh   !
So if you want a nice day filled with fun
It's a quick short trip up the old M
Not that far from   !
It's good old   !
So now you know exactly where
Other towns just don't compare
It's pointless even going there
Don't even bother'em'
Just head to

Thought you guys could fill in the blanks here with your own home town on this one. I'm sure it's not that difficult to work out the proper town though! Anyway, have fun.

NAUGHTY CHRISTMAS PART 2

Can it be done?
Another Christmas song
That sounds a bit like it shouldn't
Would you all mind,
If I passed on it this time
Or simply said that I couldn't?
What's that I hear?
You're not happy chaps?
You want a nice naughty Christmas
Well you dirty old folk
Let's give Santa a poke
And see if he'll fulfil your wishes!
Ok, Now if you recall
Last time in the hall
Santa unloaded his sack
With some heaves and some groans
And some help from Miss Jones
Who somehow got some on her rack!
But she soon cleaned it off
With the wipe of a cloth
And put it all back on show
Then after he'd thanked her
And festively spanked her
Santa said "now I must go"
"My sack's refilled, fit to burst
  With a brand new batch of loot!"
Then with ease of grace
Like a greased angels race
He disappeared right up her chute

Miss Jones in awe and wonder
Spoke with some surprise
 "I didn't think you'd fit up there
  You are quite a size"
But Santa was in trouble
Things had gotten hard
So shouted out
"BY RUCK I'M STUCK,
  FETCH A BLOCK OF LARD!"
So as lard ensued, he came unglued
Miss Jones was quite a dear
And after she pulled him all the way out, asked
"Same time next year?"

HEAR ME SQUEAK!!!

60 foot tall and covered in hair
With teeth of a shark
And claws of a bear
Muscles from Athens
Built like a house
Soars like an eagle
And roars like a mouse. squeak!

WOULD YOU BELIEVE ME?

Legend says that there lies a pot of Gold at the end of every
Rainbow! What legend doesn't say though is that at the beginning,
there is a skip full of shit! Make sure you go to the right end!

SORRY, WHAT? THINK UP MAN!

How do we form the words?
The ones we never say
The ones we hear inside our head
Almost 24 hours a day

Why do we form these words?
The ones that are never spoken
Are we so afraid of vocal crime?
Or is the volume control broken?

And should one day
We fix the fuse and crank the volume up
Will we sigh relief, or sigh with grief
And wish we'd kept it shut?

HALF AAAAAAGGGGGGHHHHHSSSSSSSSD!!!!!!

I saw a ghost the other day
Who scared me half to death!
And the spooky ghoul just 'stood' and laughed
As I gasped and grasped for breath
"W, w, what's so funny?" I finally asked
In a stammeringly, babbling tone
"Well" he said "it's just your luck"
"I'm out here on my own!"

These two were the final ones to go into this book! They're great
aren't they? This is now quite untrue!

RAIN ANOTHER DAY

Who hexed the hols?
Dashed our plans
Pushed boredom to new heights?
Flooded hopes
Of flags and floats
Drenched sunshine out of sight
Nowhere is dry
And even the plight of the superest spy
Is just 2hours action past bore
He crashes the car
Escapes unharmed
Guess what? I've seen it before!
So here's to the Great British weather
On this wonderfully grey holiday
And the man in the tux
With his endless luck
Please send some of it this way!

You guessed it, it's raining! Bank Holiday and it is pouring down!!!

For this next piece, I will be combining two branches from the
artistic tree; poetry and mime. And a 1, and a 2 and a,

       bendy
            vagina
  salty

Thank you!

AH BLESS!

Bless our souls
Cleanse our souls
Keep our souls free from pain
Kiss our souls
Love our souls
Our souls are not the same

THE DREAMS OF THE LIGHT BRIGADE

So we charged forth
Into the Valley of Death
On orders misconstrued
673 men
Our welcome was beyond all hope
Barrage after barrage of shells
From not one, but three directions
Funny to think
The enemy thought we had had too much to drink
Fine chance
We were doing our job
Doing our duty
To refuse would have been somewhat rude
Now I can see it all before me
A valiant charge, with no real hope
On orders misconstrued.

I've not been putting dates of late, sorry chaps and chapesses. This
was written 6th June 12. There you go!!!

DREAMJA VU

"Hark" the Herald angels scream
Pray you'll wake up from this dream
Where ghosts of old have pissed on hope
And redemption is a useless joke
Where time has flown then crashed and burnt
And pity pays poor for any lessons learnt
Memories? Ha, you are out of depth
You'll be lucky to remember your last breath
Gasped with panic, so filled with need
Of those bedtime stories you dared to read
That drifted you off unto this dream
"Hark" the Herald angels scream.

Gosh, that was a bit dark wasn't it? And scary! Just be careful what
you read before bed folks! Carry on reading this though. This is ok!

SOS?

She took hold of the Greengrocers cherry
Then rolled it around in her mouth
Until drawn out and firm he told her stern
"Young Lady you must take it out"
"But Sir" she quipped "Your cherry's so big
   And it feels so nice on my lips"
"Well if that's the case, then carry on
   Just don't spit out the pips"

Very nearly forgot to put these two in! Spank me later!!! Ouch!

63

FUNKY ZOO PART TWO! GET DOWN!!!

Bats abound
The cheetah's chase
The snakes just laze
While the rhino's race
A parade of penguins
Salute the bears
As the kangaroos watch
The boxing hares
The monkeys dine
Cream tea for two!
And the cats are cool
At the Funky Zoo!

CUT SHORT

A telephone call
Should consist of no more
Than one of the following three
I'm on my way
I'm running late
Or it can never be
If it goes on then it's not much fun
And starts to hurt my ear

The word Echelon refers to staggered formations of troops, possibly in battle! There you go, I learned you something today to make you gooder.

THE SING-A-SAURUS 12" REMIX

In Dinosaur Town
You will hear a sound
That is really quite bizarre
It's a bit like a wonky washing machine
Or a broken down old car
Now the chances are
You've never heard such a grumbly-mumbly noise
As the mighty Sing-a-Saurus
And his grumbly-mumbly voice
He wakes up at 8 o-clock
Sometimes just before
Brushes his teeth, has some toast
And gives a MIGHTY ROAR
Then he starts to sing
It doesn't matter what
He knows the words to lots of songs
From Opera
Through to pop
But he sings so very loudly
So that everybody hears
So make sure you take your earmuffs
To cover up your ears

I was going to lay down a backing track to this one, but have no idea
how to. If you would like to add a few licks to it and sing along, I'm
sure you will have great fun. Just don't blame me if you look a bit of
a knob!

I CAN'T ROLL YOU

A car
A boat
A plane
A tank
A truck
A train
CD, TV, MP3
HI-FI, WI-FI, DVD
So many things to have and hold
So many things you can control
With the push of a button
Or flick of a switch
From a little black box
It's so, so quick
Think of all the hours of fun
Things doing things how you want them done
Checked off your list, 1, 2, 3
Just don't point your black box,
At me.

CLICKITY FIX!!!

Quick click
All is fixed
Everything's good as new
Just as well
As I can't be arsed
Waiting for drying glue

NO WAIT, I FORGET!

The reception is deserted
So are all the floors
The windows' glass
Has all been smashed!
And replaced with wooden boards
Furniture's been upended
Strewn across the floor
This God-forsaken place
Has a brand new face
It's in a better state than before.
And there's laughter in the hallways
Sniggers in the air
Though there's not much to laugh at
No one seems to care.
No one will ever find them
They are free to run amok
They are only bound
By memories found
And a heavy duty lock.

"NO WAIT, I FORGET" was written eons ago, almost as a song! I really didn't like it (song writing is not my strong point). So, after digging it out of the folder of old, I tweaked it a little bit, shortened it, added a new ending and,,, . Oh pants, I've forgot! Enjoy.

Would you like to call me? Would you like to see me?
Could you ever love me? Would you ever leave me?
Aaawww!

CALLING DOCTOR CARLY 2

Near the end of the race
With such gallant pace
The leader gave us a smile fit for art
But he came unstuck
When he caught his foot
And sent his teeth back to the start.

I'M FOREVER PUSHING PENNIES

It's balancing right on the edge
This time it's going to fall
One or two more should do it
This time I'll keep it all.
Chances are I've spent a hundred
And got back about ten
But it's balancing right on the edge
So I'll put it all back in again

Written after a nice day at New Brighton arcades. Those penny
pushing machines are such annoyingly good fun. And yes, I did lose
all my money!!! £2 I'll never see again!

Mr Mikes' handy hints

Don't let resentment dance on your grave, just stop caring now!

You know you are old, when you have to hold on to something when
you sneeze.

FREE FALLING

I'm free falling
I can see the sky turning to a dark shade of grey
There's someone calling
But I can't hear a word that they say
I'm caught in a stalemate
A wonderful catch 22
Whilst scavengers are mauling
Trying to find a piece of mind to chew.

FLOWER POWER

Would you care to enlighten us?
What is in store for your next shout?
Is it all a bit hush-hush?
Or are you going to let it all out
You once flew your flag depicting power
But now stand alone
Like a dying flower

YOU BET I WILL

I'll cut off your air
So you can't breath
I'll banish sleep
So you can't dream
Destroy all hope
So you can't pray
In all I'll really mess up your day attached

SATANS WHY?

The Devil looked up
From down below
And gave a hefty sigh
Pondering on the question
Why does nobody like me?
Why oh why oh why?
Is it because I'm ugly
With these orrible orns on my ed
Or simply the fact I'm an orrible chap
And really can't wait till you're dead.

LORDS A-WHY?

A Lord looked down
From up above
And gave a beaming smile
Pondering on the thought
Everyone seems to like me
I can't think why?
Is it because I'm so noble
And made lemmings and sofas and fairs
Or is it the fact I'm a damn nice chap
And you all want a place upstairs

Well you can't have one without the other now can you? Satan's day
12th 6th 12. Just as well it's not the 12th of the 12th 12, twice the
amount of Omens! Eeeeeeeeeeeeek! Aaaaaaaaaaaaarrrrrrrgggghh!
Oooooooooooooooooohhhhh! Just a tad bit of over acting there!

SO LONG

A chill is hanging in the air
The sky's afraid to speak
A storm is heading in this way
She'll be here sometime next week
Fit from fighting last
Replenished to the teeth
An ambassador of all that is war
And the key to eternal peace
The barer of great fortune
For those of hope denied
And the chance of some salvation
For those of sleep deprived
You could batten down the hatches
Repent for sin and crime
But Red Snow is on a brand new watch
It's a mere matter of time

It would have been extremely rude not to have included a brand
new Red Snow verse in this book. Told you she would be back!

SPIRITS LEVELLED

Society's falling to pieces
Coming apart at the seems
Law and order have been and gone
Pack-up your hopes and dreams
The cracks are getting wider
Between the them and us
Confusion reigns in acid tones
As push is forced to shove
The levels are dividing
Their bubbles fit to burst
The spirit of a nation
Is near anarchic thirst.

CHRONOLOGICAL DISORDER

I had that Friday feeling
HOORAH!
But that was yesterday.
Then realised
My mind had lied
And it was in fact Thursday
BOO!
Then Friday came around
YAHOO!!!
But the feeling was just not there
And now it's bloody Saturday
And I really just don't care

MR MIKE PETERSON PROUDLY PRESENTS
THE INCREDIBLY EXCITING ADVENTURES OF "Dr LUSTY L TIFFOCH"
OK, THEY MAY NOT BE OVERLY EXCITING! BUT THEY ARE RUDE!

Many miles were travelled
Through Antarctic's deep snows and Sahara's hot sands
In her ongoing quest, to lay her hands
Upon untold treasure, beyond wealth or price
And an unfulfilled craving to satisfy vice
For the price she sought wasn't stolen or bought
Made of gems or precious stones
Gold played no part in this fine piece of art
It was fashioned of flesh and bones
"So what?" you are asking "Is the prize of her tasking?"
"In suspense, will you keep us how long?"
Dear reader fear not, for here comes the plot (at last)
She doth seek the "All Mighty Dong"

Some do say "Tis 12 inch long"
Whilst others argue "16!"
But it's so hard to quote, on the tales of folk
The likes of whom, have not seen.
For the "Dong" is of status
Beyond mortal man!
And of girth beyond a large pie
With thick wiry hair that covers a pair
And an all seeing cycloptic eye.
For the finder reward, they will never be bored
The "Dong" will satisfy all of your vices
And after it's done you, stretched you and numbed you
It still has a load of surprises!

But where on earth can the Mighty Dong be?
Dr Lusty must seek high and low.
Be it between a nice valley, or deep in the bush?
And just how far will she go?
It could be that the legend has flopped
Or it could be pushed hard up a creek
It's Dr Lusty L Tiffoch's job to find out
So be sure to tune in next week!

Now, in a complete reversal of roles, shock horror, this rude ditty
was supposed to be a kids verse! It was supposed to feature a
character called the Grumpy Old Guffoo! Not Dr Lusty L Tiffoch!
Dr T was created years ago, and I thought it would be a shame to
not use her, so,,,, TA DA!!! Here she is! P.s she's got a cracking pair.
I mean cracking, proper hefty!

WEAK PEEP!

Little Bo-Peep
Gave up chocolate last week
And is now having
One of her cravings
Leave her alone
Don't talk, text or phone
Or your head
She's likely to cave in.

I tried writing poetry once as well, made an even worse mess.

PHWORDER FORM
NICE LADY READERS, PLEASE USE THIS SECTION TO CREATE YOUR PERFECT IMAGINARY PARTNER!

LOOKS LIKE;
SOUNDS LIKE;
BUILT LIKE;
ACTS LIKE;
DRIVES LIKE;
COOKS LIKE;
SINGS LIKE;
BODY OF;
HEART OF;
SOUL OF;
HAIR OF;
KNOWLEDGE OF;
SIZE OF;

NICE BLOKE READERS, PLEASE USE THIS SECTION TO CREATE YOUR PERFECT IMAGINARY PARTNER!

LOOKS LIKE;
DRINKS LIKE;

REAR VIEW MIRROR!

Alice went to Wonderland
Had a wonderful show stopping farce
Then went and dropped a looking glass
And really saw her arse!

TWO SILLY BULLS

Two silly bulls
Climbed to the top of a tree
Using sticky tape, crayons and wire
Then had a quick look
Thought they were stuck
So carried on climbing up higher!

DAYS GONE UG!

Papers covering the evolution of human intelligence will now have to be completely and utterly rewritten! Recent archaeological digs have revealed that our Neolithic ancestors were not only painting pictures on cave walls, some 10,000 years ago, they were also writing a basic form of poetry. Though a lot of it is unintelligible, historical linguists have been able to translate the following;

If you're happy and you know it shout "UG!"

Humpty Dumpty him taste good!

Old McDonald had a club

Him start fire!

Things that make you go UG!

Polly blew the dinghy up (Lee, this one's for you)

76

ACES HARD

The King of Hearts
Did not like tarts
He found them dull and bland
Like crackers
Instead he said
I'd rather have
A couple of dirty old slappers.

FACED OFF

So how come now
You want to be friends
At this point in time?
As I recall
I was no friend of yours
And you were no friend of mine
So what has changed?
What's the score?
Some terribly awful blunder?
Or simply the case
That on your face
You just want another number?

Unsightly garden weeds say your prayers and prepare to feel the
might wrath and power of STRIMATRON! Come on, we all like to feel
big sometimes!

Ok, you can stop with the spanking now! Thanks! It was fun ;)

THE ALL SEETHING

Sat talking for hours
Not said a word
So much has been spoken
Nothing has been heard
I can see your face
It never moves
There's no expression
Is it all a lie? Are we all blind?
To multimedia deception!

COLLATERAL DAMAGE

I see you have a new weapon
A new way of waging war
How fantastically, brilliantly brilliant
But haven't you done it before?
Don't tell me, this one is quicker
In engaging and killing its kill
Or is it more cost effective
And will decrease the tax payer's bill?
I know, I know, it can find
One man within a crowd
And will only seek out sinners
By golly you've done us proud
So it's faster, smarter, cheaper
And a whole lot easier to manage
So let's hear it for the screaming souls
Amidst the collateral damage

Totally went off on a tangent with that last one "Collateral Damage". Initlally it was meant to have been about mobile phones and how annoying they can be. In the wrong hands! However! When the phrase "Collateral Damage" reared its consonants, I just had to re-work it. Just as well really as the mobile phone one was piffle!

Ok my time twisting, travelling buddies, on this next piece we are going to go back a few bits to the 16-bit age, if you want to. Skip a couple of pages if you want to stay here and now. It was the grandular year of 1994 if I am correct (yes I am, I wrote this). T'was a time of knowledge gone wrong, of learning gone wronger and of teaching, well that just went so wrongerer, t'was beyond hope! Little-ole-me was doing a college course and had to keep a diary (yeh right), it went a tad off the rails. Please read on. Extract taken from the 7/10/94 (told you).

DIARY OF SORTS

Day, not sure, not the first one though!

BANANA, BANANA, BANANA, BANANA etc. Sorry about that, HAHA fooled you, I'm not really.

Oh it's no good, I just can't motivate myself to put anymore down in this, "THE MEANINGLESS DIARY, FROM THE PLANET DRIVEL".

I mean, can you honestly say that you are enjoying reading this meaningless tripe, as much as yours truly is enjoying writing it? As I've mentioned before, were I am at the minute, there is no spell check fasillity. So I'm not even sure that what is ritten down makes any sense. Although things could be worse, God help us both if I were using just pen, paper and the old grey matter.

"WARNING, BRAIN IS APPROACHING CRITICAL CONDITION. YOU NOW HAVE 10 SECONDS TO STOP WRITING REPETITIVE CRAP".

Oh nearly forgot "---" this afternoon was all right, very informative and well presented, etc, etc, etc.

Day after yesterday!

IIIIIIIT'S ME.

Back once again to pollute paper and write crap.

Today we had "—" and it was good, then we had "-------" but that was boring, and I nearly fell asleep.

At dinner time I went to the shops and got my hair cut very short. But when I got back to college the dinner hall was shut. So I could not have anything to eat.

In the afternoon we had "—" which is all about business, it was all-right.

Well I think this just about kicks the arse out of it. Sorry but I'm just not cut out to write diaries. I mean I'm supposed to be putting down what my views are of this and that on paper, for you to read. In my opinion if you want to know what I think, all you have to do is ask. Whether or not you get an answer though, is a totally different matter.

And anyway, what the bloody hell are you doing reading my bloody diary? Is there no privacy these days?

Day, not sure. Skipped a few days so as not to bore you

It's here, it's now. Yes it's true. Only one thrilling instalment left. But I can't be arsed to put anything down.
I could say that "—" this afternoon was interesting for once. But I can't be arse.

I could say that I have actually enjoyed writing the last few days of this. But I can't be arsed.

I could say "Mary had a little lamb". But guess what?

On a serious note now; I remember in the instructions of this, it asked about what I hope to achieve after this course. Well now, that's a tricky one isn't it? I know, I want to be a bank manager, no I want to be a programmer, no no, I want to be an astronaut. Thing is, I haven't got a clue, I'm too busy dealing with here and now, to even consider what I might be doing in two years time. So please who ever, or whatever you are, reading this now; please do not approach me and start asking me stupid questions about my future.

Because I do not know. I mean, tomorrow I could get massacred by "GIANT KILLER HAMSTERS FROM THE PLANET SUNFLOWER SEED. AAAAAAAAAAAAAAAAAAAGGGGGGGGGGGGGGGGGHHHHHHHHHHH HHHH"

All events written in above text are as close to how it was originally. I may have changed a couple of punctuation marks here and there and left out a couple of bananas, but apart from that, it's tickedy-boo! And no, I didn't finish the course. Nor was I set upon my big hamsters.

STAND UP, STOOD DOWN

I watched somebody die last night
A slow and painful death
I suppose really I should have done something
As he did his best to catch his breath
But I just sat and watched
I couldn't laugh or cry
And like the others in the room
We just watched this poor man die
In all it took just minutes
Maybe longer than it ought
But in the end he knew he'd lost
And so he cut it short
Embarrassed laughs and half arsed claps
Saw him to his grave
And for a minute, maybe two
There was silence on the stage

Written with regards to a comedy gig I went to.

WHICH WAY DOES THE WIND DO BLOW?

THE FANTASY

Elleyenore Devinour oh-so surpassed chic
If it needed doing, it was done by last week
She'd tread the boards, till the boards were worn out
And if something was wrong it was wrong and no doubt
Her style was a nature so delicately pinned
And she smelt like a rose if she ever broke wind

THE TRUTH

Elleyenore Devinour was a lazy old cow
If it needed doing, someone else did it 'NOW!'
They'd then tread the boards, till she told them to stop
And if they stepped out of line, my life did she strop
Her style was a mismatch of garbage come art
And she smelt like a dirty old dumpster
Whenever she cracked a fart

Wow folks, that was the first ever dual purpose verse that I have ever written! (I think) And wasn't it great!

Pn: Ell-EYE-nor Deh-VINE-nore

Imaginary friends categorically and without doubt do not exist! They are extremely honest though.

I was once told I had a face for radio and a voice for canvas!

LITTLE BLOW-PEEP

Little Bo-Peep
Had fallen asleep
Half way through her shift in the morn. Tut tut!
So Little Boy Blue
Did what he could do
To wake her up with his horn
He started afar so as not to start
Her lazily grazing sheep
But Peep merely yawned
So he took his big horn
And slapped it across her cheek
Far from calm
Peep woke-up with alarm
And so the story goes
Though it was bent she took half of its length
And gave it a couple of blows
Now widely awake
Peep realised her fate
Had been spared a long stint on the dole
While Little Boy Blue had a smile on his face
And his horn was as stiff as a pole.

30TH July 12
WIP

With horn removed/ Peep was back on the job/ And as a thanks for waking her up/
So pleased was Bo, so the story goes/ She gave it a couple of blows/ "Thank you"
she said /"For waking me up/ "Oh dear" she said/ On waking up/ But got no
response/ So he moved in real close/ She had a look/ And snatched it out of his
hand/ "Oh dear" she said "that's not much / So her sheep did a bunk/ And gave her
the hump

A RIGHT ROYAL LICKING

The Queen of Hearts
She did like tarts
She could eat them all day long
With cream, such fun
Or nothing on!
Now this is where things could go wrong
For if your mind is pure
Unstained and true to form
You'd think she liked a nice sweet dish
And that and nothing more
But just a sec!
That's not the case
That simply isn't true
You've read this much
You mucky pups
How this ends is up to you!

X thank you and goodnight!

Who is Bill Posters, and why will he be prosecuted? What has he done?

Right, that's your lot now! Haven't you got TV's to watch or something? Go on off you pop!

Ooops! A slight hic-up in the making of this has resulted in a couple of extra pages! I ain't got a clue what I am going to put in here, but I'll do my best for you.

BOOKENDS

Two little bookends
Sitting on a shelf
Neither could read a page
So they missed all the chances
Of tears, laughs, romances
And just drifted apart
With old age

LET US PLAY GRACE

I tried to do, what I could do
But do was not enough
I tried to say what need be said
But words were just rebuffed
Now games are played in childish ways
To try and do out done
But when you're not a child
These games are not much fun
So I'll throw my dice one last time
But it's not to take first place
I'm too old to play this silly stuff
I'm just bowing out with grace.

Take that to the grave Blinky!

These next two pages are entitled "Echelons' Scraps". This is merely a brief look at some of the bits and bobs that did not make the final cut. Basically because they just didn't work! I did try to find homes for them, but to no avail.

It looks like scientific ideas about when the evolution of human intelligence will all have to be rewritten, due to remarkable new evidence that has

Theories surrounding the point in time in which our Neolithic ancestors first started writing have

A recent archaeological dig has thrown new light onto when our Neolithic ancestors may have first gained the ability to write.

Archaeological Scientists

The world of Archaeology and Prehistoric Human Evolution has been completely

The evolution of neolithic human brain

Scientists, who are studying the evolution of human intelligence, have been left somewhat bewildered after a recent excavation unearthed a treasure trove of priceless art that questions the level of intelligence our Neolithic ancestors had.

unearthed not only Neolithic cave paintings, but also what looks like Neolithic poetry written on the walls as well.

Recent excavations have unearthed a treasure trove of priceless art that questions the level of intelligence our Neolithic ancestors had. For it now turns out, not only did they have the ability to convey their thoughts into cave paintings, they were also writing in a basic form of poetry. Below are some examples;

Don't be too personal

Ok, so how many more years of evolution is it going to take, before flying insects realise if they go left or right, they might get out?

The eagerly awaited prequel to "Lunacy and Tripe"! Available in all good shops soon, maybe! And some bad ones as well.

Apart from 12 hours passing by, nothing happens overnight!

In this edition, I have done my best to fill each and every page with as much "Lunacy and Tripe" as possible! Hence the title! I really do hope you enjoy it and thanks for looking!

Humpty Dumpty sat on the wall/ With a little mouse on the handlebars/ carried plasters and And now that feelings gone/ As now it's Saturday!

Somewhere out there/ Maybe behind a tree/ Is the Grumpy old Gufoo/ Who is very hard to see/ Somewhere out there/ Is the Grumpy old Gufoo/ He is such a grumpy mumbly bum That he has hidden himself from you/ Now the Grumpy Gufoo can run really fast

Faster than a / Quick look!/ Is that him zooming past?/ He's getting faster and faster and faster/ No sorry, it's not him/ t's just an incredibly fast badger/And he can hide away really well/ He disappears like magic/ Quick look!/ Is that him hiding there?/ Under that old log? No sorry, it's not him/ It's just an incredibly big hedgehog/ Because he has had his tea

I think that he had pasta/ Bleach is deadly/ Can you run really fast?/ A new state of confusion

Is now in place/ THIS IS NOT A REPEAT! I REPEAT, THIS IS NOT A REPEAT!

In a bakers shop/ A long time ago/ Something didn't go quite to plan/ The silly old baker made to much dough/ When making a gingerbread man/ He couldn't make another/ There wasn't enough for two/ And he really couldn't waste it/ That just wouldn't do/ He jumped around and scratched his head/ And gave him a big ginger dog/ A nice big gingerbread dog/ "It's going to come out wrong!"/ Then he had a strange idea/ "I'll give him a gingerbread dong"

So carefully he crafted/ A mighty ginger shaft/ "Oh me, oh my! What shall I do?"/ Then he had a sly idea, and gave a wicked grin

So Billy-the-Scape Goat has fled the field/ Leaving you in the lurch/ Pray tell your next intention/ To seek salvation from a church?

How do we form the words?/ The ones we hear in our head/ The ones that are never spoken How is it we hear them/ As clear as day/ Yet the volume control seems broken/ What if we spoke out these words!/ Told it how it is/ Would the world be a better place?/ Would it cure Your picture painted

Was he pushed, or did he jump? This, my friend, is a sombre question that has remained unanswered for many a generation. Was it a conspiracy, if so who was behind it? An act of vengeance, if so why? Or was it just a simple accident? Whichever way you look at it all we know is this; Humpty Dumpty was in a pretty bad way after his 'fall'.

Of late I have been looking into the old riddle that is this; did Humpty Dumpty jump or was he pushed? (I have a lot of time on my hands). Now it just so happens that yours truly has come across some rather interesting CCTV footage and previously unreleased witness statements, which may

Shhh lets tiptoe round the house. Try not to make a sound, sssshhh!. A little mouse has lost his way. And needs to be found/ So we can't be very noisy/ Or we'll scare the little mouse So let's be very, very quiet/ And tiptoe round the house./ Let's tiptoe to the kitchen To try and find the mouse/ He has got to be here somewhere/ Somewhere in the house Ssshh, is that him over there/ Underneath the chair

t was in fashion now, it was oh-so last week/ Such is her manner she'd turn garbage to art/ For Lord, help the mere mortal who dared cross her path/ And seek out salvation if you chose not to laugh/ At her jokes, oh-so funny yet so callously dry/ She would smell like a rose upon cracking a fart

YOU'VE DONE THE CRIME, NOW PAY THE FINE!

If all good things come to an end (like this book)
Are the bad just waiting in line? (like this book)
To bring us back down to earth?
Then hand out "Happy Fines?"
Are these nasty little buggers
Going to wreck our happy day?
That my friend is up to you
And if you really want to pay!

Seriously now, that is it! Thank you and Goodnight!!! You have been
wonderful!!! X

P.s How's Grace? I heard she fell.